A SONG FOR UNCLE HARRY

A SONG FOR UNCLE HARRY

by *David Kherdian*

ILLUSTRATED BY NONNY HOGROGIAN

PHILOMEL BOOKS • NEW YORK

Text copyright © 1989 by David Kherdian. Illustrations copyright © 1989 by Nonny H. Kherdian. Published by Philomel Books, a division of The Putnam & Grosset Group, 200 Madison Avenue, New York, NY 10016. All rights reserved. Published simultaneously in Canada. Printed in the United States. Book design by Nonny Hogrogian. Library of Congress Cataloging-in-Publication Data. Kherdian, David. A song for Uncle Harry/by David Kherdian; illustrated by Nonny Hogrogian. p. cm. Summary: A young boy relates his special friendship with his Armenian uncle. ISBN 0-399-21895-5 [1. Armenian Americans—Fiction. 2. Uncles—Fiction.] I. Hogrogian, Nonny, ill. Title. PZ7.K527Sk 1989 [Fic]—dc19 89-3700 CIP AC

1 3 5 7 9 8 6 4 2

Dedicated to the memory
of my mother and father
Uncle Jack and Aunt Blanche
and Mike Kaiserlian

A SONG FOR UNCLE HARRY

CHAPTER ONE

I have known my uncle for as long as I can remember. Ever since I was born he lived on the same block as us. We lived across the street from each other and at opposite ends of the block, but it was a short block and had a dead end.

I'm twelve now, but I still remember the toy drum he bought me for my fourth birthday. It was rimmed all around with real leather and had Indian signs in different colors, and the drum even had a name: *Kotochino*. I liked the wooden sticks best of all because without them you couldn't bang the drum and make the noise a drum makes. The first thing I did was hand them over to Uncle Harry. "Show me," I said.

My uncle beat the sticks against each other, then on the sides of the drum and then on the head of the drum, which was what he was supposed to do in the first place. My uncle is very funny and he knows it.

"Like an Indian, Petey?"

"Be Chief Kotochino!" I exclaimed. I don't think my uncle ever thought about Indians before, because the next thing he did was put the strap over his head and begin singing, *Good Morning, Mr. Zip, Zip, Zip.* That was the first time I had ever heard Uncle Harry sing that song, but every time he came over to our house after that he would sing that song for us, whether I asked him to or not. My mom and dad think Uncle Harry is funny, too. So does my little sister. But I guess he's funnier for me than for anyone else, and I guess that's because he's probably my favorite person in the whole world.

CHAPTER TWO

It's hard to think about Uncle Harry without thinking about his Model A Ford. In a way they go together. We're Armenian, you see, and my uncle is the only person from the Old Country that I know of who owns a car. My father can't even drive. If it wasn't for Uncle Harry I probably wouldn't even know what the inside of a car looks like when it's moving. But I suppose if I didn't have my uncle's car to crawl around in, I'd find some other car.

Cars have the neatest smells inside. I mean, you can *really smell* the cushions, and when you close all the doors, if you're alone, it's like being in a two-room house, and you don't have to use a door to go from one room to another—you can just go right over the top of the seat. It's a neat way to change rooms when you're playing with someone. If you're in the back, you've got the rear window all to yourself, and if you're in the front, you've got the steering wheel. You can pretend to drive, and there's no harm in pretending it's an airplane, either, because it could just as easily be one.

The happiest days of my life are when Uncle Harry comes over and says, "We're going fishing tomorrow, Petey. Get your poles ready and dig up some worms."

Fishing is my favorite thing in the whole world. I like it better than working on my fort, playing marbles or cars, going swimming, or even going to the movies. I guess I like all these things almost as much as fishing, but fishing is special because you can't just do it anytime you like, and it is also extra special when Uncle Harry takes us because it means an all day outing. And of course it includes a car ride out of town—all the way to a place called Thompsondale, which is a place without a single house anywhere, only this wonderful river that never stops moving, with big trees growing almost right out of it. I have my own favorite tree which has a trunk you can sit on right over the water, and that's where I sit and fish.

Uncle Harry always lets me bring one of my friends, and it's usually my cousin Sam, because he likes to fish almost as much as I do. Although all we ever do is fish from the minute we get there till the second we leave, we do run back and forth from our spots to see how the other guy is doing.

While we're fishing, my mom and dad spend a lot

of time picking grape leaves, which they use for wrappers when they make *sarma*. They always pick enough for my mother to can, so we can have *sarma* anytime we like in the winter.

Uncle Harry fishes sometimes, and sometimes he picks grape leaves, but mostly he lies down by the water and closes his eyes. "I'm listening to the water," he says. "It soothes my nerves. It reminds me of the homeland, and it tells me life is endless, without beginning or end. Only when I am here do I know that nothing has been lost, that my people are still alive and that we will meet one day on the bank of another river. Not this river, but another river—far, far away."

My uncle has a way of saying things that I just can't forget, even if I don't always understand what the words mean.

CHAPTER THREE

My uncle was gassed in the First World War when he was with the U.S. Army in France. That's why he's always at home and doesn't have to work or anything. He just draws his pension because he's too weak to hold down a job. So I didn't figure he'd ever move, leave, get a job, get married, or anything else. I just took my uncle for granted. I thought he'd always be right where he was, and he'd always be my best and favorite uncle.

The thing about Uncle Harry was that he never asked me any embarrassing questions about my actions. When I cut myself, or stepped on a nail, or just got tired and hungry, I'd go over there and tell my uncle everything and get a peanut butter and jelly sandwich and a glass of milk. Whereas, if I went home, my mother would scold me, *then* feed me, and chances are she wouldn't let me go outside again, and she'd probably even want to *talk* to me.

One time when I was little, I hurt myself and

Uncle Harry taught me how to read time on a clock. Sammy and I had been throwing bottles against this brick building and all at once a piece of glass flew back and sliced open my finger right down to the bone. Naturally I ran straight to Uncle Harry's, where he cleaned my finger and bandaged it and then made me a peanut butter and grape jelly sandwich.

Then with the toothpick he took out of his mouth he pointed to the hands on the clock he keeps on the kitchen table, and he said, "Do you see the two hands?"

"Hands?"

"The things that point at the numbers."

"No, I see one."

"That's right. That's because it's exactly twelve o'clock."

"Oh."

"Both hands are on the hour. But at other times only the little hand is on the hour. Twelve, one, two. . . ."

"Eight o'clock is *Inner Sanctum*," I interrupted.

"That's in the evening on the radio, but what time does school start?"

"Eight o'clock in the morning. But there's only one eight on your clock, Uncle Harry. How come?"

"The day is divided in half. There is twelve o'clock noon and twelve o'clock midnight."

"Isn't there any difference?"

"The sun is the difference. The sun is time, not the clock. Man made a clock to read the sun with. The first half, up to twelve, the sun is coming up; the second half, starting with one, the sun is going down."

"We're in the second half."

"That's right. It's five minutes after twelve."

"But the big hand's on the one."

"Yes, the big hand keeps track of the hour. The little hand *is* the hour. Do you see?"

"I think so."

"The big hand has to go all the way around to twelve, and when it does, then the little hand will have gone to here—and it will be one o'clock. Have you heard of twelve-thirty?"

"Yes."

"That's here. It means thirty minutes after twelve o'clock."

"What's quarter after?"

"Here," Uncle Harry said, and pointed to the three.

"And the next time after that, when the big hand gets to twelve again, it will be two o'clock!" I exclaimed.

"So—now you can read time."

I was amazed. I *could* read time. I looked at my Uncle Harry, and then I looked back at the clock and *read* it. I read the time! When I looked over at my uncle, we both gave out a big laugh. I had learned to read time and I hadn't once noticed that my finger was throbbing.

CHAPTER FOUR

I love my father, but we hardly ever did anything together. He went to work before I got up for school, but not before he had stoked the fire with coal. In the cold winter months I would dress in front of the register where the heat comes up and every once in a while I would remember that my father had built the fire before he left. I was glad he was able to do it because it took everything I had just to stand there, shaking and trembling in front of the register, while I froze to death.

But I wouldn't see my father until just before supper, when he would walk into the kitchen door wearing his heavy Old Country coat. I call it an Old Country coat because it feels like it belongs to the past. He'd walk to the door leading to the cellar, open it and hang his coat on a peg inside the door, and then he would go downstairs and change his clothes. He's always pretty dirty because he works in a factory sweeping floors—and he smells like a factory too. I think he tries to keep that smell in the cellar, but it always creeps upstairs. Maybe it's just gotten into his skin over the years and can't be washed away in the shower downstairs.

After he had changed and walked upstairs he would turn on the radio and listen to Gabrielle Heater giving the news. You have to be grown up to understand what this man Gabrielle Heater is saying, or to *care* about what he is saying. I remember him saying once that there was going to be another world war if we weren't careful. Gabrielle Heater didn't sound very careful to me, although he was trying to be calm. But you could just tell he was upset down underneath and very serious about his concerns. Whenever my father listened to him, his face kind of sucked itself up into a serious wrinkle of worry. Maybe it had something to do with my father not wearing his teeth when he listened to the news. He was probably giving them a rest before supper.

Sometimes it seemed like the only other thing my father did when he was home was read the Armenian newspaper. Armenian is the only language he can read, and he doesn't read it very well because he has to move his lips when he reads, and he sounds out about half of the words. It is very distracting if you are trying to read yourself, not that I ever read in the living room. I read in my bedroom and play in the dining room, where my dad does his reading and listening to the radio. His reading doesn't bother me when I'm playing and for some reason my playing doesn't bother him when he's reading. But then my father never used to notice me much. I think it was because he was usually thinking about the Old Country, and all the members of his family that were lost in the Massacres. The difference between my dad and Uncle Harry was that Uncle Harry had a plan.

You see, Uncle Harry had a sister who managed to escape to another country, and Uncle Harry was always trying to bring her to America. My father mostly brooded, but Uncle Harry was always thinking and making his plan.

CHAPTER FIVE

They say my father was very generous once. He had saved all his money to send to his mother, who had survived the war with Turkey and was stuck in the Old Country. When she died, he kept on sending money to his brothers and sister who were left, hoping they would come to America. But in the end they stayed in Armenia too. So by the time I came along he had gotten pretty stingy with his dough, not that he had much to spare.

For example, I really don't have much trouble getting my weekly allowance out of my dad, but I have to beg for it. Well, not exactly beg, but you know what I mean. I have to stand there in front of him while he gives me that amazed look. "Is it Friday *again?*" he asks. It never fails. That's the first thing he always says.

Sometimes I lose my temper—if he makes me feel like I'm begging. But usually at this point he smiles, to let me know he's teasing. Then he reaches into his pocket and takes out his change, but he keeps his fist closed. When he does open it, he makes sure that only he can see what's inside of it. Then, one by one, he takes out the coins that make the amount go over 25¢. Then he closes his fist again and sticks it out in front of me. When he opens it palm up, I have to take the coins out of his hand. When I started to grow older, it made me feel crummy. It made me want to earn my own money. It also made me want to complain to my mom.

"He's playing a game," my mom would say. "Why can't you play with him?"

"It's his game, not mine, and I don't like it. I never know if he's going to give me my allowance or not."

"Never mind, he loves you."

Whenever she said that, I knew the argument was officially over.

Uncle Harry isn't stingy at all and never has been as far as I know. Of course I'm his only nephew, and my dad is his only cousin in this country. The same is true for Uncle Harry. He's my father's only cousin in this country. I bet they didn't know that Uncle Harry sometimes gave me a nickel—and once in a while, a dime. Just for nothing. Once he bought me something on the street. I'll never forget that day as long as I live. It was last summer when I was eleven years old. I was playing outside with our neighbor's pet rabbit. They've got one black and one white rabbit that they keep in a cage. I've got their permission to let them out of the cage one at a time because they know I'll look after them.

I love rabbits more than any other animal in the whole world. They're not only soft and fluffy and cuddly, but they have these ears that look make-believe, and pink eyes and noses. And they don't walk, they bounce, and they nibble with their mouths when they eat, and they nibble with their noses when you hold them in your arms. They don't exactly *love* to be held, but they don't especially mind, either.

Anyhow, I was putting Tammy back in the cage—she's the white female—and about to take out Gabby, who's the black male, when I heard our phone ring. I like to answer the phone when I'm inside the house, but I don't usually pay much attention to it when I'm outside and hear it ring. Of course I don't usually hear it when I'm outside. This time I not only heard it, I knew something was wrong. My mother calls this thing I've got intuition. I've got it pretty strong, I guess, because I usually know who's calling. I closed Tammy's cage and ran inside the house.

"Yes, yes," my mother was saying into the phone—in English. "I understand, of course, of course." And then she hung up.

"Who was it?" I asked.

"Uncle Harry's tenant," Mother answered, "the old man who lives in the apartment upstairs from Uncle Harry."

"Did someone die?"

My mother gave me this look. It was a combination of *how* could you know, and *why* do you know? I stared back at her.

"Go find Uncle Harry. He's probably at the coffeehouse on Milwaukee Avenue," she said.

"First tell me who died."

"Who said anyone died!"

I stared at my mother and didn't move.

All at once she started crying, which made me feel pretty bad because I felt like it was all my fault.

"Please, Mom," I pleaded.

"It's Zabel," Mom said, and turning away, she took out her hankie and covered the top half of her face.

Zabel is Uncle Harry's sister. She was the one Uncle Harry was trying to bring to America from Beirut, but he was having trouble because of the quota system. She was the only member of his family he had left. All the others had been killed by the Turks during the time of the Massacres which happened after the war.

"When you find him," my mom was saying, "tell him to come here. That's all. Just tell him to come here. Do you understand?"

"Yes," I answered in Armenian. "I understand."

I didn't have a bicycle so I ran. It was eight blocks away, but I didn't stop once—and I never slowed down, either. I had this idea that I had to get there as quickly as possible. Now that I think about it, I can't remember passing any of the houses or buildings along the way. I was really scared, I guess. No one I knew had died before, and of course I didn't know Aunt Zabel, either—I only thought I knew her, and only because Uncle Harry talked about her all the time. She was his *hope*. That's how he put it. When I was really young I couldn't figure out what he was talking about because he would say the word *hope* almost as often as *Zabel*.

"This is my hope," he would say. "When Zabel comes we will make a new family. She'll marry, have children. We'll be together again, under one roof, as we were once before, long ago. The same stars shine on this country as the country of home. Why should life not continue?"

I think it was because of her that he bought a two-story house on our block. And she was the reason he lived on the top floor. "Children shouldn't climb stairs," he would say. "They might fall down. Also, it's bad for pregnant women, you know. A family should remain close to the earth. If you are near the earth it will support you."

"Then why don't you live on the first floor until Zabel gets here?" my mother once asked.

"I need to be nearer the heavens, so our Father will answer my prayer. If I move downstairs my mission will weaken."

Uncle Harry didn't like living on the second floor. "It is one thing to sleep on the roof," he would say, "it is another to *live* up there."

"Ouf, Harry," my mother would exclaim, but then she would grow silent. I couldn't tell if she was remembering the flat-topped roofs of her childhood home, or the days when she was a wandering orphan after the war with Turkey.

When I had reached the corner of State and Milwaukee, I stopped. The coffeehouse, which was an unpainted store-like structure, was directly across the street. I was suddenly afraid, and I knew all at once the deep and true sadness of the meaning of the message I was about to deliver.

All eyes turned and looked at me when I opened the door. The room was filled with smoke. Most of the men were seated at tables, some reading, others playing backgammon or cards. There was a feeling of loneliness in the room. I felt confused and lonely, too. I watched a man in a white apron pick up a tray from a back counter that held a *jezveh* and several small, white cups.

Even though I was staring straight ahead as I walked, I knew which of the eyes belonged to my uncle. I stopped in front of him. "Sit here," he said, and as I sat down he pressed my shoulder gently. He walked to the back of the coffeehouse, and I saw him pick up the phone and speak into the receiver. His expression didn't change, but when he hung up he let his arm fall with the earpiece still in his hand. The man I was seated next to began talking to me in a soothing voice, but I was unable to listen to his words. I was staring at Uncle Harry, and I had a big lump in my throat.

CHAPTER SIX

The next thing I remembered, my uncle and I were standing on the sidewalk in front of the coffeehouse. "Don't you like this sun, Petey," Uncle Harry said. "Even the sidewalk is golden, just look."

The air above the sidewalk was shimmering, but it didn't look golden to me. Just then I heard the bell of the ice cream man, who was a block away and headed in our direction. I looked up at Uncle Harry who was smiling at me. It was only then that I remembered his sister. I was no longer scared, I only wondered why Uncle Harry was smiling, but just then he started to whistle at the ice cream man. Uncle Harry can't whistle at all—no Armenian man that I ever saw can—but I was more than glad to whistle for him. Pushing my tongue back with my two fingers, I let go with as loud a whistle as I had in me.

Uncle slapped me on the back and motioned me

toward the ice cream man, who had pulled up alongside the curb. "Tell him what you want."

"Eskimo bar," I said to my uncle, loud enough for the ice cream man to hear.

"Also me," Uncle said in English to the man, which really surprised me because I didn't think he would even know how to eat an ice cream bar.

The ice cream man pedaled away. I undid the wrapper and wound it around the bottom of the stick. Uncle Harry did the same. I could tell it was his first Eskimo bar. We stood on the sidewalk in front of the coffeehouse and began eating our ice cream bars.

Uncle Harry did fine with his first bite, and it struck me funny watching him eat an ice cream bar in the street, wearing a suit with a hat on his head. Pretty soon he started tilting his head, probably to get his moustache out of the way. "How am I doing?" he asked.

"It's about to drip onto the stick. You'd better lick it," I said, "like this."

Uncle Harry bent over at the waist and began licking the melting ice cream. I wondered if his hat was going to fall off. "This is a good American invention," he said, "ice cream on a stick. But difficult."

We looked at each other and smiled. Uncle Harry

had chocolate all around his mouth. He said, "How would you like to take a ride?"

I looked at my uncle in disbelief. I had never taken a ride with my uncle just for the fun of it. "Sure," I said.

We got in his car, but instead of driving off we sat quietly inside and rolled down our windows. Uncle smiled when he looked at me, but when he turned away the smile left his face. At first I didn't know if I should say anything or not, and then all at once I knew I didn't have to say anything. We were together, and a family knows when it is good to speak and when it is good to be silent.

I'm glad I didn't ask him where we were going after he started up the car, because when we turned the corner on State Street I knew we weren't going home. Pretty soon, we were headed out of town, past the cornfields and the farmhouses and barns, with pigeons circling the silos and the ploughed fields, and after a while I noticed that we were driving along in the direction of Thompsondale.

It was funny to be going somewhere familiar but with a completely different feeling inside. Instead of the usual excitement about fishing, I was glad to be sitting quietly in my seat next to my uncle. We were having this time together, and although I didn't understand all the feelings that were going on inside of me, I knew that this was an important time and that I needed to be quiet and just let what was happening happen.

It wasn't long before we pulled off the road and drove down to the river.

"We've never come here like this before," Uncle Harry said, "just the two of us without the family."

"Yes," I answered.

"Should we just take a walk?"

"Sure," I said.

"As we walked along the river towards where we always fished and had our picnics, Uncle Harry began singing. I recognized the song right away because it was one of our church songs, but I didn't know the name of it. Our choir sings all kinds of songs, but I never learned the names of these songs. All I know is some priest by the name of Gomidas wrote all of them, or at least most of them. They're mostly these old songs that Gomidas learned by traveling from one village to another in the Old Country. So I guess they're village songs. He did this before the First World War, because after the war, when the Turks had massacred almost all the Armenians there were, Gomidas lost his mind and couldn't write any more songs. He's a big hero with the Armenians because he put together all these village songs and he also wrote the holy music of the church, which is supposed to be very hard to do and rare.

Uncle Harry was looking out at the river and singing as if he were talking to the trees and the sky and the river itself. I took his hand and when I did, I realized he was crying, and then I started crying, too. I don't know if I was crying because Uncle was crying or because the song was so sad, or because I knew that his song was for Aunt Zabel dying.

We sat down beside each other on the bank and stared at the moving water. Armenians have this thing about water that is pretty hard to explain. Maybe all people have it. I don't know. I only know that something happens when we get near water, and it doesn't really matter what kind of water it is. I guess Uncle had wanted to come here to let himself feel bad about his sister. And I'm glad he did, and that he brought me with him.

I had a question, but we sat there in silence for a long time before I asked it. "What is dying, Uncle Harry?"

Uncle didn't answer me at first. He just stared at the top of the trees across the river. The sun was in the upper branches and the breeze was blowing the limbs and the leaves back and forth. All at once Uncle reached down and cupped water with his right hand. "All of this river is the life of Man," he said. "Do you understand? But what I am holding in my hand, this is my sister, removed from life. Now I put her back again," and saying this, he thrust his

cupped hand back into the water. "There is no death, there are only possibilities. The possibility of my sister. The possibilities *for* my sister—this time, in this life—are finished, but the river of life flows on. Do you understand?"

I nodded yes, because I thought I *did* understand, but as I looked at the water I wondered what Uncle was feeling.

CHAPTER SEVEN

We never talked with each other about his sister again. She was like a secret between us. I knew that my father's sister would never leave the Old Country, now that they were settled in Armenia. So Uncle Harry had lost the last member of his family, and I had lost—or so I thought then—my last chance to have an aunt.

I used to wonder what it would be like to have an aunt that I could talk to in the way that I talked to Uncle Harry. I didn't like confiding in my mom because she was nosy and always wanted me to do things her way. "*Petey, do this. Petey, do that.*" And the same with my pop. One time I confided I wanted a bike. He couldn't—or wouldn't—understand why it was important to me. "Where can you go with two more wheels that you can't go to now," was how my dad put it.

"I can get there faster," I shouted, "a lot faster!"

"What's your hurry?" my father shouted back.

"I can't wait!" I hollered again.

"You can't always have what you want the minute you want it," he said.

But Uncle Harry was interested in everything I did, and like I said, he didn't criticize or praise what I did, he just listened and smiled, and never got tired of my chatter—which I must admit I sometimes saved up just for him.

One time I mentioned to him about a mother bullhead I had seen with her little babies while I had been crabbing in Island Park. There must have been fifty of them. Well, maybe not fifty, but a lot. They were all around and mostly underneath her, but they would keep floating up and down along her sides, as swiftly and jittery as she was slow and calm. The mother bullhead and her young had come up nearly to the surface. I followed them as they swam along the bank, and for some reason this hardly bothered the mother at all. I couldn't get over how beautiful the tiny, baby bullheads were. They were each about the size of a tiny thimble, and just perfectly formed, with whiskers and everything.

I don't know what made me mention this to Uncle Harry, but I'm sure glad I did because he got almost as excited as I did, so I was able to tell him all about it, right down to the details.

"Imagine," Uncle Harry said, "fish looking after their young just as we do. Who would have thought?"

"What did you think they did when they had babies, Uncle Harry?"

"I don't know. I guess I never thought about it before."

"Did you think they just swam away after they had them?"

"That must have been what I thought."

"Was the mother teaching them how to feed, do you think?"

"Yes. Maybe so. Maybe so. And protecting them. Did it look like she was protecting them?"

"Oh, yes. They never went more than a few inches from her side."

"That's why she was fearless. There is something that happens between mothers and babies."

Uncle Harry looked off into space, and I wondered if he was thinking about the massacres again. Or Aunt Zabel. Suddenly he turned back to me and said, "You must make a drawing. I want to see what you saw."

I was really surprised. Uncle Harry knew I liked to draw because whenever my mother took me visiting with her I always drew pictures because it was the only thing I could do while I waited that wasn't boring. But this was the first time I ever heard him say anything about my drawings. He got up from the kitchen table we were sitting at. We never sat together in the living room because it was too formal—we always sat in the kitchen, the same way you would with a pal.

I started my picture right off with the mother bullhead. I made her almost as big as the paper, and as black as I could possibly make her. I placed her babies all around her, with a few off to the side to indicate that they would get lost if they weren't careful, because this is how it looked to me. Uncle Harry didn't sit down. Instead, he went to the bread box, and, as he did, he asked over his shoulder, "Peanut butter and jelly?"

"Sure," I answered, without looking up.

"Grape, or pineapple-peach?"

I had to give that some thought. "I never had pineapple-peach before," I said at last.

"Then have it."

By the time he came over with our sandwiches, with milk for me and coffee for himself, I was just about finished.

"Just as you said," Uncle Harry exclaimed, and slapped the side of his face with his open hand, the way all the old Armenians do when they are surprised or overcome by something. He propped my drawing against the milk bottle and we just sat there staring at it while I drank my milk and Uncle Harry sipped his coffee.

CHAPTER EIGHT

On my next birthday Uncle Harry gave me a water-color set. All the presents he gave me were special. This one was also surprising. Before I could say anything, Uncle Harry said, "Remember when you drew the bullheads?"

"Uh-huh."

"You've forgotten that the pencil couldn't make them black enough? Remember?"

I nodded yes.

"Well, I thought, there's another problem. Bull-heads have brown in them, too, and you can't mix colors with pencils. I've seen you try. But with water colors, well, it's possible, but I think it's going to take work, hard work. It's up to you to figure out how to do it."

I haven't told you yet that my Uncle Harry believes in work, which surprised me when I first heard him talk about it because he doesn't work himself—can't work on account of his illness. And he moves slowly, the way most Armenian men do—and, well, when *I* think of work I think of all the men in the factories and foundries in our town, sweating and slaving away. But I gradually figured out that that was not what Uncle Harry was talking about. He was talking about using your brains to figure things out, not quitting when you get a little tired or bored, or whining when things go wrong. Stuff like that.

So I knew I was going to have problems with the watercolors. But he knew something that I didn't know then, that I needed to work at something new where drawing was concerned. Before I had gone at it strictly with pencil and paper, but now I needed to go at it with water colors, which were harder to work with.

"If something sits in one place too long it dies," Uncle Harry was saying from somewhere behind me. I almost didn't hear the words, probably because I didn't know what he meant.

CHAPTER NINE

One day I realized that Uncle Harry was the only Armenian man I ever talked to besides my father. There are about two hundred Armenian families in our town of 67,000 people, and most of them live on the north side, mostly in our neighborhood. We are like a big family. Everyone knows everyone else. The adults are responsible for us. They love us and care about us, but they also don't care to talk to us. We really don't want to talk to them either, because if we do they might tell us to stop. Or go home. Or be quiet. Which of course they sometimes do anyhow. I mean, they don't seem to be really interested in us, and I suppose we aren't really interested in them. They love us and we respect them, and that is enough. Almost.

All this came to me one day while Uncle Harry and I were sitting together on the back porch. I realized that day for the first time that Uncle Harry was different. And it was only then that I began to wonder why he was different.

There was a sunflower between us on the porch that Uncle had placed there. I don't know where he could have found it because he doesn't grow sunflowers. Of course he never takes a walk without coming home with something. He considers it laziness and a waste of time to walk just for the exercise; it is necessary to find things and bring them back home, even if they aren't things you can eat or use for some definite purpose. For example, he collects things just to look at them or study them. Then, after a while, out those things go, to make room for a new batch of things to look at and study. His kitchen table and other countertops are always loaded with pebbles, branches, nuts and berries, broken objects that once were parts of things; and outside, his house is surrounded with large rocks that he has "found" on river banks.

One day when I was little I got mad at him for stealing rocks from the river. "Stealing!" he roared. "Who am I stealing from?"

I had to think that one over, but finally I came up with an answer. "God!"

"Oh, Him," he said. "He's got plenty." Uncle laughed and so did I. "Besides," he continued, "God doesn't care if things get moved around. None of us own anything—including ourselves. All we can do with things is make new combinations, which are soon dispersed—which then make other new combinations possible."

While Uncle was talking that day on the back porch, I was reaching into the sunflower and taking out seeds to crack and eat. Somehow, the way it so often happens with Uncle Harry, I lost track of time and the next thing I remembered Uncle Harry was saying, "We are making our own sunset." He seemed to be staring up at the sky.

At that moment I was cracking a seed between my teeth, and I looked over at Uncle Harry and then down at the sunflower. Only then did I realize what he was looking at: the setting sun. Suddenly, it hit me, or bubbled up from inside me: the sunflower was the child of the sun. Nature made herself over, in patterns that were surely endless. I would probably miss most of them, but I had seen this one, thanks to Uncle Harry.

Uncle reached over for the first time and took a seed from the sunflower. He cracked it between his teeth, and I cracked one between my teeth. The sun, the seed, me, my uncle, the sky, and the flower— everything was one, nothing was separate, and Uncle was right, Aunt Zabel was alive. We just couldn't see her right now.

CHAPTER TEN

From the time I was seven years old I began sitting with Uncle Harry on his back porch. It is an unusual porch in that it seems to have been added on to the house after the house had long been built. There is also an inside porch, and both porches are joined to the same landing, with separate doors for each.

There are twenty-one steps, straight up in a line. And facing the steps is a gate that leads to Uncle Harry's garden. The fencerow, except for the gate area, is lined with cherry trees. These are Uncle Harry's pride and joy, and also the source of his greatest frustration because the moment the cherries turn ripe the birds fall on the trees from all directions and eat every last cherry they can find.

Uncle Harry loves his cherries because he can't grow pomegranates, figs, apricots or grapes "worth eating." "Son a ba gun Veeskonsin veddher," he always says, in his longest English sentence. *Son a ba gun* doesn't exist in the Armenian language, but he likes the expression so much he's obliged to speak English more often than he would like. My father has his own expression in English for the Wisconsin weather that all of the Armenians seem to hate. "Lousy veddher never see." The *never see* part he uses on various occasions, but the words *lousy* and *weather* are always used in the same breath, and they are always spoken in English. The word in Armenian for weather seems to be air. The air *this* and the air *that*. One thing is certain: there is no bad air or water in Armenia.

And of course both the air and the water of Wisconsin are definitely not very good.

"Don't forget the mulberry trees, Uncle," I reminded Uncle Harry once when he had gone too far with his complaints about Wisconsin. The mulberry fruit, called *tout* in Armenian, is perhaps the most Armenian fruit of all, and even I'm aware that the mulberry tree has something to do with the making of silk. In the Old Country, the fruit was used to make spirits. And of course no one had to tell me about the quality of the fruit itself because it is my favorite. There are a number of mulberry trees scattered throughout our city, all of them growing wild, even when they belong to someone's lawn. Americans do not seem to value the fruit, which ripens on the branch, and is wet and sticky to the touch and has to be eaten instantly. It becomes bruised almost at once if it is picked and not instantly eaten. The only correct way to eat mulberries is in front of the tree.

But Uncle Harry has no mulberry tree, so the cherry trees are a compromise—have to be a compromise—because they are not figs, apricots, pomegranates or loquat, the other Armenian fruits that can not be grown in Wisconsin. And added to the compromise of growing cherries is the furthur compromise of sharing the bounty with the birds. It goes without saying that Armenian fruits do not have "predators," and so the fault of the "cherry problem" is blamed on the weather, which is blamed on Wisconsin, which is the fault of the country itself. This is the Armenians' way of addressing their sadness about the past and the losses that went with it, which are too painful to go into directly.

The air here does not issue from the blue vault of heaven, the water is not as sweet as the flavor of *tout,* and the fruit itself—Uncle Harry's only edible fruit—is always being attacked by pests.

Finally, unable to bear his losses or the insult any longer, my uncle bought a bb gun and began shooting at the birds. "Son a ba gun birds, vy dey don't go bodder Veener his trees, ha?"

It is very difficult for me at such moments not to laugh. If only his next-door neighbor's name had not been Weiner. For some reason the W doesn't exist in the Armenian language, and V makes a very funny W, especially when there are a number of them strung out in a single sentence.

"Don't laugh!" Uncle would shout—and not necessarily at me, but to all the people who looked at him just a little funny because of his accent. "Do not forget that there is a language behind this language, that makes *this* language come out funny," he would say in a sentence that was almost as funny as his accent. "My tongue may be crooked, but my brain is not."

CHAPTER ELEVEN

I don't visit Uncle Harry as often in the winter as I do in the summer months. I don't spend as much time outdoors in the winter, and so I don't get hurt or into trouble nearly as often. And of course we can't sit on his back porch, like we do in the summer, which are the times I most enjoy being with him.

But one day in November, when I stopped at his home on my way back from school, he seemed especially happy to see me. "You come just right time," he said in English, which he had been practicing up on lately.

"What is it, Uncle?" I asked, as I followed him into the living room. We seldom sit in the kitchen in the winter, nor do we ever eat peanut butter and jelly sandwiches; only fruits and nuts. There's always a bowl of assorted nuts with a nut cracker on a low table before the fireplace. That's the other thing: the fire is always going.

As far as I know, Uncle Harry has the only home

with a fireplace in our neighborhood. "Why do you think I bought this house?" he asked me one day. We were sitting in front of his fireplace, staring at the burning logs and enjoying their warmth. As so often happens, he had read my mind. I had also wanted to ask how he got his wood, but I didn't want to break the silence, and this time he didn't read my mind. I was sure he got the wood the way he got nearly everything. "I find," he would always say when I discovered something new in his home or garage. But I don't think he ever accidentally stumbled over anything, which is how I found things—although I got better at finding things his way as time went on.

Uncle Harry has a way of locating things at the moment they become loosened from their surroundings but before they have been discarded. "I find new use," is the way he puts it, and as far as I am concerned he is recycling things before they get lost. Not everyone sees it that way, though.

After I had sat down across from him that day in November, I noticed that in place of the usual bowl of nuts, there was a different, larger bowl, and inside it a mound of chestnuts. They were different from the kind I collected, smaller and duller.

"Remember these?" he asked, interrupting my thoughts.

"Not really," I answered.

He laughed at the puzzled look on my face before speaking again. "We find together. Remember? Johnson Park."

"Oh!" I shouted. "Sure, now I remember. I had to borrow your gloves to pick them up."

"Well, they are edible."

"What!" I exclaimed. I looked at Uncle Harry, then the chestnuts, and then at Uncle again. I collected the bigger chestnuts every autumn. They were something you treasured because of their hidden beauty—but no one had ever spoken of *eating* them!

I remembered now that I had looked at the husks of the smaller nuts and thought they were unusual. I wasn't even sure there were chestnuts inside because they didn't have any weight to them at all. They weren't like the hardcased spiked chestnuts I was used to. Their prickly fur reminded me of porcupines, except that I had never tried to pick up a porcupine.

"They come from the only edible chestnut tree in *whole town*," Uncle Harry was saying, emphasizing the last two words in English.

I was staring at the bowl of chestnuts, remembering the sunny autumn day we had collected them. We had loaded two whole gunnysacks full that Uncle Harry had locked up in his trunk. Uncle got up from his chair and took down the popcorn shaker that he always kept next to the fireplace. After he had placed it on the table, he took out his pocket knife and began cutting crosses into the chestnuts. When each one was cut he dropped them into the metal shaker until the bottom was completely filled. "Now we cook them," he said, as he extended the shaker over the coals.

Now I knew that they were edible because although he was known to do some pretty strange things—at least in the eyes of others—I had never known him to cook something he didn't intend to eat.

They seemed to puff up and pop open from the heat of the fire—which was of course the idea—but when I grabbed one from the shaker it was too hot to hold.

"Give it a minute," Uncle Harry said. "And then peel it."

I had never seen the inside of a chestnut before. "Now?" I asked, after I had peeled my first one.

"O.K.," he replied in English and laughed.

I bit into a completely new experience. "It's not like a nut," I said, my mouth half full, "or like anything else."

"Do you like it?"

I nodded my head.

"Good. Not one dime cost it. How you like that!"

We sat all afternoon, cutting, cooking and eating chestnuts, taking turns as we went, and eating them just as fast as they were cooked, which, I knew, was not the way he would have done it if I were not there. I was enjoying the chestnuts and he was enjoying me, and, of course, the thrill of finding and cooking food that didn't have to be paid for in the usual way.

CHAPTER TWELVE

That was not the first time I had sat with Uncle Harry in his living room in front of the fireplace. But it was the first time we had cooked something together. I knew that he cooked his meals over the fire sometimes, especially lamb and vegetable shish kebab, because the skewer he used was also kept beside the fireplace. I didn't think they cooked like this in the Old Country, but I do know they cooked this way in America in the olden days because I saw a picture in my schoolbook of a woman cooking in her fireplace. Uncle Harry liked cooking this way because it made the food taste better.

Uncle Harry is good at enjoying things. For example, he and I both like to collect things. I collect coupons, bottles for deposit, box tops for prizes, and things like that, and Uncle Harry collects—or finds—things to look at and things to eat. The difference is that he enjoys and uses the stuff he collects immediately, whereas I am always collecting things and saving them forever, or waiting in anticipation to use them.

Nothing is ever as good as I imagine it to be, or as neat as it is supposed to be. Especially when it's something announced on the radio, like on the Jack Armstrong show, where I once sent for a pedometer. I mean, I drove my mom crazy waiting for it to show up in the mail. It finally came after three weeks. My cousin got one, too, at exactly the same time because we had sent in our coupons together. And so we put the pedometers on our belts and started walking around and timing how far we had gone, and all that. But we got bored with it almost at once. For one thing, you couldn't fall down or anything or you'd break it, and I probably never went out of the house even once without falling down at least two or three times. I mean, if I want to sit on the grass, I don't just sit down, I crash down, stomach first. So my pedometer and Sammy's were put away somewhere, and unless we go on a long hike or something, I guess we'll never use them again.

So that's just an example of the way I'm always waiting. Uncle Harry gets full measure out of everything he finds. And he finds things for me, as well as for himself. He is always giving me things he finds on his walks: marbles, a block of wood to whittle or use for my fishing lines, coupons you get from Raleigh cigarettes that you can trade in for something else, odd-looking stones for my rock collection, and so on.

Another thing that Uncle Harry finds wherever he goes is food. Not only hazelnuts and black walnuts, but vegetables and things that have to be cooked. I mean, food like you would buy in a store. I had known about Uncle Harry finding food for a long time because people would talk about it. Uncle Harry was known for this, along with all the other things he was known for. He wasn't exactly a character, like Willy and Kookoolala, who went around with kids' wagons or gunnysacks, collecting junk. Kookoolala, for example, carried an axe with him.

Uncle Harry goes everywhere only as himself, but he is a sight sometimes, carrying branches and stuff in his arms, with his pockets bulging with other things he's found. I thought it was mostly pretty neat, which is why I would get so mad at my mom and dad when they would say, "I wonder what Harry has found to eat today." They would emphasize *found* to make it sound like *steal*, if you know what I mean. As far as I was concerned, Uncle Harry was perfect, and if he *found* things, as they put it, then that was the perfect way to do it.

I guess it was for this reason that I got mad at my parents and did what I did. I asked Uncle Harry if I could go with him the next time he went looking for food. The look he gave me made me sink into my highcuts. "On one of your walks," I blurted out, but all he said was, "What do you mean?" It suddenly occurred to me that Uncle didn't plan his life, he just lived it. Gathering food and stuff as he went along was as natural for him as breathing.

"Dandelion leaves," I said, which was the first thing that popped into my head. "Let's find some."

"Dandelion leaves!" Uncle Harry exclaimed, and smiled.

I smiled back, relieved.

"As a matter of fact, this is the perfect time. April. We'll need two bags, one for you and one for me. You have to pick them young, when they are tender. So, my boy," Uncle Harry said, pulling two bags from the cupboard, "let's get going."

And off we went. We marched down the stairs, turned the corner and headed for the J. I. Case offices, whose lawns were loaded with dandelions.

I couldn't believe it. Here we were with our bags, like a couple of D. P.'s—displaced persons—on maybe the busiest corner in town, picking dandelions. I thought I would die. But I don't think Uncle Harry even noticed. In fact, the next thing he said made me feel even more conspicuous. "This way we clean their lawn at the same time we are getting food to eat."

Although he told me to pick only the young plants, I was so nervous from being noticed by everyone that walked by that all I could think to do was fill my bag as quickly as possible.

Uncle Harry threw out most of my leaves when we got back home, but it didn't matter because we had more than enough for the two of us. Eating dandelion leaves wasn't much different, or any better than eating spinach. But there *was* a difference, although I didn't know at first what that difference was. It was because we had picked them ourselves, and also we had practically discovered them, for although they were there in open sight, everyone else walked by, not noticing or caring. But not us. We stopped and picked them.

And that little bit of difference was all the difference in the world. Up until that moment I had always taken food for granted. I just assumed it would be there on my plate when I needed it. When I raided gardens with Sammy and some of my other friends, it wasn't food we were looking for so much as it was adventure. There was always the chance we'd get caught. We enjoyed the food because it was "stolen." And because we had "stolen" it together, we enjoyed eating it together. Picking dandelions was different because it was intentional, and intelligent—and out of the ordinary. And it was done in broad daylight.

I mean, you had to know what you were doing, you had to know what was what, and then you had to know how to find it. Which meant you had to know what things looked like. Uncle Harry could *see*. He saw what others missed, or didn't bother to notice.

"How do you know when they are ready to pick?" I asked Uncle Harry that day.

"By looking," he answered without lifting his head. "How do you know when something is cooked?"

"I don't know."

"By tasting! Aren't you learning anything practical at your Garfield School?"

We were back at Uncle Harry's house. I had cleaned the leaves and was standing over the stove, waiting for the water to come to a boil.

"Don't dream!" Uncle Harry said at my back. "When you dream, you must plan. Don't dream while cooking, like when you stare out window at Garfield School while teacher talking."

How did he know that was what I did?

"Now I teach you cooking, but nobody can teach you to listen and to see. These are two most important things for understanding. If you can listen and you can see, already you are an artist, already you can begin to think. Then life is your school. Understand?"

Uncle Harry had never spoken to me in this way before. I felt like he was preparing me for something, which was definitely not the feeling I ever got at school.

Uncle had stopped talking.

I stared down at the water and tried not to dream. All at once I saw that the leaves were alive. Everything was. The kettle, the gas flame, the stove, the salt shaker—everything! I looked down at the leaves again and my mind became very still. It came to me then—not as a thought, but as the simple truth—that everything was perfect. I couldn't say why, and yet I knew that I didn't need to know why. It just was!

CHAPTER THIRTEEN

I didn't know it, but Uncle Harry had an idea. It was definitely connected to the time we gathered dandelions. I had always enjoyed drawing people and animals, and even sofas and chairs and houses, but now I had a reason to draw—a purpose, you might say. If I could draw a plant, first from life and then from memory, I would really know each plant and I'd be able to spot them anywhere. And it was thrilling to see how many I could find and draw.

But I have to confess that this wasn't my idea. At least not at first, because the next time I went to visit Uncle Harry he gave me this really neat drawing tablet and suggested I start making drawings of things that could be found and eaten. He already knew that I liked to make lists and keep track of things, and I realized later that he was looking for a way to "harness my energies," as my homeroom teacher once said to me. I'd rather run than walk, fall down than stand up, squirm than sit straight. It drives my teachers crazy. "If you don't harness your energies, Pete, I don't know what's going to become of you."

That was how she put it. I mean, what was supposed to become of me?

"What should I draw first?" I asked Uncle Harry. I was warming up to the idea, but I was still a little scared and uncertain.

"How about the chestnut tree. It doesn't look like the kind that isn't any good for anything." This made me smile because I prized both kinds of chestnut trees. But I knew what he meant—he was being practical. "You think you can recognize it now, but don't be so sure," he went on. "You might walk right underneath one and not know the difference."

"Not if I've drawn it!" I exclaimed, which, the minute I said it, made me laugh. I realized that I was beginning to see the practical side of all this myself.

Uncle Harry smiled.

"And underneath the drawing of the tree," I went on, growing excited, "I can put two drawings of the chestnut, one with the shell, and then next to it the chestnut inside the shell. That way, anyone looking at my tree will know what kind it is."

Uncle Harry nodded his approval.

"Should I put a drawing of the other kind of chestnut tree on the page facing this one?"

"Maybe you should put only edible trees and plants in this book. So you can identify them."

"I'll call it *Edible Trees and Plants I Have Observed*, or something like that."

"I think that sounds perfect."

"I think maybe it does."

CHAPTER FOURTEEN

I got so busy with my project that I lost all track of time. I was busy exploring, identifying and drawing. I even got interested in going to the library, where I found some really neat books on trees. Then, in the next week, I went to Uncle Harry's twice to show him my drawings and ask him some questions, but both times he was gone. His house was shut tight. After my second attempt I became a little puzzled, and maybe even a little suspicious.

Finally I asked my mom if she had seen Uncle Harry lately.

"He's gone to Chicago."

"Chicago! He never goes to Chicago. What's in Chicago?"

"A young lady."

"A what?"

"A young lady," mother repeated. "I think he's getting engaged."

I stared at my mother, who got herself busy cutting vegetables for dinner.

I went to my room and closed the door. I couldn't believe it. What was going to happen now? Would I still see Uncle Harry? Of course! But it would be different. It *sure* would. What would she be like—my aunt? Horrible! She was going to take Uncle Harry away. What if they moved to Chicago, then what? I couldn't bear it. I threw myself down on the bed and tried not to think. I lay there like that for what seemed like eons, and then, almost without my knowing it, Uncle Harry's words came to me, words I hadn't understood at the time. "If something sits in one place too long, it dies."

Probably Uncle Harry had always planned to get married but just hadn't let anyone in on it. It had probably been his secret all along. If I had been prepared I might have felt differently about it. But I hadn't been. I guess sitting in one place too long wasn't what was going to kill him. But at that moment I felt like his not being able to sit still was about to end everything we had ever had together.

CHAPTER FIFTEEN

I didn't see Uncle Harry for maybe two weeks. One day, when I got home from the library, he was in the kitchen talking to my mom. He looked happy but preoccupied. I sat down and stared at him for a while, and then without saying anything to anyone, I walked to Sammy's house to see if he wanted to blast some milk bottles on La Salle Street.

That Saturday, during breakfast, my dad said to me, "Pete, isn't it time you had your own bike?"

I was flabbergasted. One, I didn't think my dad would ever consider buying me a bike, and two, the idea of owning my own bike had become a dream. I had been waiting to share this dream with Uncle Harry at the next opportunity, not knowing that the opportunity would never come.

My mouth must have been hanging open, because when I didn't answer, Father went on, "You need to get outside the city limits if you want to find edible plants to draw."

"And you can't do that without a bicycle," Mother joined in.

I would have formally agreed, except that I could see that it was all set already. They had decided. And probably they had read my mind. Maybe they were more intuitive than I gave them credit for.

My dad isn't much of a talker, unlike Uncle Harry who can discuss anything under the sun. But here he was talking to me, offering to get me a bike, and even understanding why I needed it.

CHAPTER SIXTEEN

The day before I got my bike, Mother announced, "Tonight your Uncle and Aunt Charlotte are coming for supper. Go inside and clean your room. . . ." This was how she broke the news about Uncle Harry getting married.

Without waiting to hear any more, I went into my bedroom and threw myself on the bed. I was staring at the ceiling, but I don't think I could have told you what color it was even. The thoughts were going in my head, so fast and crazy I couldn't keep track of them. I was not only feeling miserable, I was feeling cheated. Also tricked—though I couldn't figure out exactly how I had been tricked. Or by whom.

I didn't realize just how crazy my thoughts were becoming until my mother knocked on my door and walked into my room.

"They're here."

"What!" I exclaimed, and leaped out of bed.

"Uncle Harry and Aunt Charlotte," my mother

answered, stony-faced. "Change into something nice, and wash your face. Hurry!"

Everyone was in the living room being social. We only use the living room for social occasions, which means it doesn't get used often enough to seem like a part of the house. I always feel like I am walking into a room for good behavior, and that was how it felt then.

At least they weren't sitting together. That was my first thought as I stood at the door, half afraid to go inside. "Hello, Uncle Harry," I said, forcing myself to speak.

"Petey boy," Uncle Harry said, "this is your Aunt Charlotte." I turned toward Aunt Charlotte, which was a mild relief because although I had been looking straight ahead at everyone but her, I had been trying to catch a glimpse of her out of the corner of my eye. Her hair was done up in a bun in the back, like all the other Armenian women I knew. It was parted in the middle. Her dress was bright red, with large, yellow roses from top to bottom. She had a hankie in one hand that kept going up and down, like a bird trying to escape from its captor. The smile on her face looked like it had been put there by someone else. I walked over and shook her hand, which was the custom.

She held my hand and patted it with her other hand. Each time she did, her hankie fell across my wrist and made it tickle. "Such a handsome boy," she exclaimed. "He takes after his father."

My father was short and bald. I wondered if she was trying to tell me something.

"What are you learning in school?" she asked, as I backed away but stood in front of her, which was also the custom.

I felt like saying that my real teacher was Uncle Harry, but I held my tongue. "I don't know," I answered.

I looked over at Uncle, who had a smile on his face I had never seen before. "Aunt Charlotte gives piano lessons," Uncle said, which seemed to him to explain something.

"I hear you're a little artist," Aunt Charlotte continued. "I'm sure there's a good future in commercial art."

"I don't know about that," I answered. I didn't feel like telling her that I wanted to be a painter.

"First get your gold bracelet," Aunt Charlotte said, which is an expression that means to make a profession. "And mark the words of your elders," she concluded, "someday you will value our wisdom." She turned toward Uncle Harry and smiled. It was like the smile on Uncle Harry's face, only different. I mean, they were different smiles but they belonged to each other.

"My father's getting me a bike to help with my

project," I said. I was emphasizing project to let Uncle Harry know that I could get along without him if I had to. But he didn't seem to hear me.

She turned now and smiled at me. The interview was over. I backed to a chair on the other side of the room.

"It's time for another toast," Mother announced. Everybody stood up with their half-finished glasses poised in front of them. I took my shot glass of *raki* from the tray—the only one cloudy from being mixed with water.

After the toast I sat back down in my seat. When I looked up from staring at my glass, I noticed that Father was staring at me. All at once he winked, something he had never done in my whole life.

The others were laughing, and when I looked at Uncle Harry I let myself feel happy for him, which for some reason helped me to feel less sorry for myself.

CHAPTER SEVENTEEN

The next day my dad and I walked all the way up State Street to Rice's Bicycle Shop, where we got my bike. It was a used one, which was okay with me because it was polished up pretty spiffy, and it was the biggest, greatest, most wonderful thing that had ever happened to me. It was red with cream borders. The seat was black leather. It even had mud guards.

As we headed for home, me on my bike (I just couldn't make myself walk it) and Dad walking, we continued with the conversation we had begun on the way to the bike shop. I'd ride ahead and then circle back to my dad, and by back and forward pedaling, stay abreast of him while I kept my bike in balance.

Without mentioning names, Dad was telling me how it was with people. That at different times in our lives different things are called for, and that we have to be ready for changes, because that's the only thing we can count on—change! "You may think that Uncle Harry has lost something," Father was saying, "because you feel you have lost something with Uncle Harry. But that is not how it is. You have gained an aunt. But you can't know that until you first *know* your aunt—and that takes time."

Somehow, as father talked, I began to see everything a little differently, and the day on the river with Uncle Harry came back to me, and I saw still another aspect of what he meant about nothing dying. Things change form. When something disappears, it only means it has become something else, which it couldn't have done if it had just stayed what it was. Uncle Harry was right, nothing lasts forever, or ends completely.

But still it was one thing to know something, or have a feeling for what it meant, and another thing to put it into practice.

"Father, what is love?" I asked, when we both had been silent for a long time.

"That's a hard one to pin down, Pete, but I know one thing. It can't exist without sharing."

All at once it hit me. Love is as big as everything that exists, but love changes and *has* to change if love is to remain. For a long, long time Uncle Harry and I shared something precious, and now I was sharing something new with my father. When I looked over at my dad he smiled at me in a way I had never seen before. Maybe it was the way I saw it, but I think it

was more than that. I felt that he had put something inside me with his smile.

I raced ahead on my bike, and then slowly circled back, but this time when I got even with Dad we didn't talk, so I repeated the maneuver over and over again, enjoying just being with him without needing anything else.